The Long Weekend

The Long Weekend

For Ripley James, my sandcastle partner – T.H.

A Red Fox Book

Published by Random House Children's Books
20 Vauxhall Bridge Road, London SW1V 2SA

A division of Random House UK Ltd
London Melbourne Sydney Auckland Johannesburg and agencies throughout the world

Copyright © 1993 Troon Harrison
Copyright © 1993 Michael Foreman

1 3 5 7 9 10 8 6 4 2

First published in Great Britain by Andersen Press Ltd 1993

Red Fox edition 1995

Printed in Hong Kong

RANDOM HOUSE UK Limited Reg. No. 954009

ISBN 0 09 930249 7

The Long Weekend

Troon Harrison and Michael Foreman

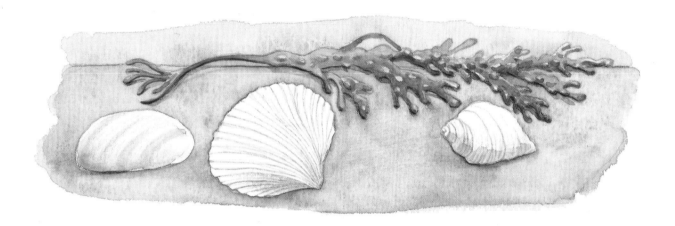

Red Fox

IT WAS summer and James was having a birthday. He was going to be five years old which was easy to remember because it was all the fingers on one hand. "James," said his mother, "What would you like for your birthday? Would you like to have a picnic with your friends and eat hotdogs? Or, would you like a trip to the zoo to ride on a camel? Or, would you like to go to the beach for a long weekend?"

She said that a long weekend was three days all in a row, and each one of them was a holiday.

James went away and thought. He thought lying down in the tall grass and white daisies. He thought sitting in the cool, green shade underneath the picnic-table and he thought lying on the hot boards of his treehouse.

He thought about hotdogs and mustard and ants and then he thought about camels and their big, flat feet. Last of all, he thought about a long weekend, which would be three whole days at the beach.

Then, James went back to his mother and whispered in her ear. He had a loud, tickly, kind of whisper and he said, "Mummy, for my birthday I want a long weekend."

ON THE first day of the long weekend, James and his mother walked down to the beach early in the morning. The sand was smooth and clean and when James took off his shoes, his feet could feel how cool it was. Mummy said that the tide had come up in the night and washed the beach.

JAMES had brought his toy cars to the beach. He sat down and began to build in the sand. First he built two long, thin hills and in the valley between he built a town. He put his fire-engine in the fire-station and made a garage where cars were repaired. He built roads over the hills and made a tunnel through them for the lorries. His break-down lorry cruised the busy roads looking for cars to tow. His fire-engine dashed out of the station with its red paint shining in the sun.
Mummy said she could hear the siren wailing.

When James and his mother went home, their shadows were long and jumpy in the sand. Little waves were rising higher up the beach as the tide came in. As darkness fell, they washed away the town in the valley and flooded the tunnels in the hills. They washed the beach clean.

ON THE second morning of the long weekend, James and his mother came down to the beach to find little birds calling along the water's edge. James began to build again. He built five round hills with valleys in between. He planted some trees. He dammed one of the valleys and filled it with water to make a pond where ducks could swim. He had brought his farm animals and he put them to graze on the hills. He fenced them in with walls of pebbles.

In the valley, James built a farmhouse and planted a garden and an orchard, where children played. James imagined hanging upside-down by his feet. Then, he built a road for the tractor to roll along, around the hills and across the top of the dam, carrying hay to the barn. The hay was full of dried flowers and prickles and it smelled of summer. Early in the morning, the cock crowed at James's farm. Mummy said she could hear it.

W HEN James and his mother went home, their shadows were long and wobbly. The waves came up the tractor road to the farmhouse. They flooded the pond and licked at the five round hills.

ON THE third day of the long weekend, James and his mother had the whole beach to themselves. James sat down and started to build in the sand.

First he built a great, steep hill and then he put a castle on the top of it. He built towers and walls with pebbles for doors and sea-shells for windows. He made flags and stood them along the battlements. Then he built a moat around the bottom of the hill and he filled it with water from the edge of the waves and set a wooden drawbridge across it.

NEXT, he planted a deep, green forest over the hills, for the deer and rabbits to share with a solitary unicorn. Through the forest he built a road for knights to

ride along in their shining armour. James imagined riding with them, on a black horse with a golden flag fluttering in the wind.

THEN James noticed that little waves were creeping over the sand. They inched towards his moat. James took his spade and dug a harbour just where the waves were emptying into the moat. A fleet of pirate ships came in with the wind and the tide and tacked with billowing sails beneath the ancient castle walls. As the ships drew near, trumpets sounded from the castle walls.

THEN, the drawbridge was slowly lowered and the crowd surged forward. A boy stepped out of the crowd and boarded the biggest pirate ship. As the trumpets sounded their fanfare, the pirates cheered and the fleet set sail.

James asked Mummy if she could hear the sound of the trumpets as they slowly died away. She said she could.

WHEN James and his mother went home their shadows were long and fluttering on the beach. The long weekend was over and so was the best of the summer.

The tide was rising and large waves crashed over the harbour and against the castle walls. The flags and battlements went swirling into the water.

JAMES was five years old. In his pocket he had two shells, a pebble and a piece of seaweed. He told his mother that he was going to keep them very carefully, perhaps for a hundred years, perhaps forever. That way he would always remember the long weekend.

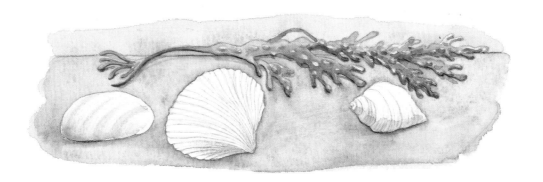

Some bestselling Red Fox picture books

THE BIG ALFIE AND ANNIE ROSE STORYBOOK
by Shirley Hughes
OLD BEAR
by Jane Hissey
OI! GET OFF OUR TRAIN
by John Burningham
I WANT A CAT
by Tony Ross
NOT NOW, BERNARD
by David McKee
ALL JOIN IN
by Quentin Blake
THE SAND HORSE
by Michael Foreman and Ann Turnbull
BAD BORIS GOES TO SCHOOL
by Susie Jenkin-Pearce
BILBO'S LAST SONG
by J.R.R. Tolkien
MATILDA
by Hilaire Belloc and Posy Simmonds
WILLY AND HUGH
by Anthony Browne
THE WINTER HEDGEHOG
by Ann and Reg Cartwright
A DARK, DARK TALE
by Ruth Brown
HARRY, THE DIRTY DOG
by Gene Zion and Margaret Bloy Graham
DR XARGLE'S BOOK OF EARTHLETS
by Jeanne Willis and Tony Ross
JAKE
by Deborah King